W9-BBB-431

STEPLADDER STEVE PLAYS BASKETBALL

SPORTS BOOKS BY C. PAUL JACKSON

For Younger Boys

BIG PLAY IN THE SMALL LEAGUE
CHRIS PLAYS SMALL FRY FOOTBALL
LITTLE LEAGUE TOURNAMENT
LITTLE MAJOR LEAGUER
PEE WEE COOK OF THE MIDGET LEAGUE
STEPLADDER STEVE PLAYS BASKETBALL
TIM, THE FOOTBALL NUT
TOMMY, SOAP BOX DERBY CHAMPION
TWO BOYS AND A SOAP BOX DERBY

For Older Boys and Men

High School Sports

BASEBALL'S SHRINE:
The National Hall of Fame and Museum
BUD BAKER, HIGH SCHOOL PITCHER
BUD BAKER, RACING SWIMMER
BUD BAKER, T QUARTERBACK
BUD PLAYS JUNIOR HIGH BASKETBALL
BUD PLAYS JUNIOR HIGH FOOTBALL
BUD PLAYS SENIOR HIGH BASKETBALL
FULLBACK IN THE LARGE FRY LEAGUE
JUNIOR HIGH FREESTYLE SWIMMER

Professional Sports

BULLPEN BARGAIN
HALL OF FAME FLANKERBACK
MINOR LEAGUE SHORTSTOP
PENNANT STRETCH DRIVE
PRO FOOTBALL ROOKIE
PRO HOCKEY COMEBACK
ROOKIE CATCHER WITH THE ATLANTA BRAVES
SECOND TIME AROUND ROOKIE
SUPER MODIFIED DRIVER
WORLD SERIES ROOKIE

STEPLADDER STEVE PLAYS BASKETBALL

by C. Paul Jackson

Illustrated by Frank Kramer

HASTINGS HOUSE · PUBLISHERS

New York

Copyright © 1969 by Cook-Jackson, Inc.

All rights reserved. No part of this book
may be reproduced without
written permission of the publisher.

Published simultaneously in Canada by
Saunders, of Toronto, Ltd. Don Mills, Ontario

SBN: 8038–6688–7

Library of Congress Catalog Card Number: 68–31693
Printed in the United States of America

Contents

For all the boys who feel awkward
when they begin playing basketball.

STEPLADDER STEVE PLAYS BASKETBALL

STANFORD STATE PLAYS BASKETBALL

CHAPTER ONE

New in Town

STEVE REYNOLDS made sure the collar around his pet's neck was snug without being too tight. He snapped a long chain leash through the collar ring. The other end of the chain was fastened around a palm tree in the Reynolds back yard.

"I hate to do this to you, Fluorescence," he said, "but I just could not have you following me."

The animal looked at him. It seemed to Steve that her eyes held accusing mournfulness. "It won't be for long," he said. "I'm just going to the store for Mom."

He straightened up. Steve Reynolds lacked a month of being eleven years of age—and lacked a bare half-inch of being six feet tall. Mates at the school he had attended in northern Georgia had always needled him about his height and gangling awkwardness. The kids down here would probably do the same, maybe they would be worse than they had been up home.

"Up home!" Steve thought aloud and shook his head in disgust. "Home is *here!* You have moved to Florida, you are not just visiting!"

He left his pet and walked rapidly toward town.

In the middle of the second block he heard someone yell, "Swish! Through the net—if there was a net! That makes me eighteen points. A long one and a short shot next turn and I'll have another game!"

A hollow sound, another, then a different *thump.* A voice wailed, "Look at that! Right in and then out again!"

Steve Reynolds came to the sidewalk end of a wide concrete drive. Three boys were taking turns throwing a basketball at a metal ring fastened to a backboard on the garage.

The stocky one with light brown hair darted across to grab a rebound of the ball that had bounced off the rim to one side. "Watch this one!" he shouted.

He arched the ball toward the basket, using both hands. The leather sphere banged against the backboard, then slanted down and hit the rim of the basket. It rolled around and around and finally dropped through.

"How's that for calling it?" the stocky boy stuck out his chest. "Just call me 'Deadeye Dick'!"

The ball rolled toward the taller of the two other boys. He picked it up and dribbled to a spot farther from the basket. "Our coach at camp told us any shot that went into the basket could not be called a poor shot," he said. "But he also told us we would make more baskets using good shooting form. Like this."

Steve Reynolds watched with admiration as the boy dribbled twice and moved smoothly into a graceful leap. At the top of the leap he pushed the ball one-handed toward the basket. It dropped through the ring without touching rim or backboard. Then he dashed in with catlike quickness, caught the ball on the first bounce and dribbled from beneath the basket. He leaped again and laid the ball feather-light against the backboard above the metal ring. It slanted off the wood down through the circle. The player caught the ball as it came down.

"Call me 'Winner Win,'" he said. "Two points for the long shot and a point for the short one give me 21."

'Winner Win' tossed the ball toward the boy

who had not had it since Steve watched. This boy was slender and not as tall as either of the others.

The pass to him was not hard or wild. He just lunged at the ball too late, barely touching it before it rolled down the driveway toward Steve.

"Just call *me* 'Fumbling Fred'!" The slender boy clutched his short blond hair with both hands and grimaced. "It sure does not look as though this game is for me!"

Steve Reynolds picked up the ball. He used only one hand to grasp the pebbled leather. He drew back to throw and knew the motion was awkward compared to the movements the other boys had made, even the lunge of "Fumbling Fred."

"Don't just heave it," Fred shouted. "Shoot a basket!"

Steve Reynolds hesitated. He wondered if he seemed as gawky as he felt. Well, the worst they could do was to laugh—and laughter was bound to come sooner or later. He nodded and grinned.

He bounced the ball once. It came off the concrete higher than he expected. His huge hands went out, but he made more a half-fumble than a good catch. He did not really have a good grip of the ball when he let fly at the backboard.

There was very little arch to the throw. The sphere banged hard against the backboard. It hit no more than two inches above the support that held the metal ring, came fast off the boards and hit the front edge of the rim. It bounced to the back of the ring and dropped through.

"How *about* that!" Fred let out a whistle. "Man! It's more than fifty feet from the sidewalk to the garage!"

"That is what you call a Long Tom!" Deadeye Dick nodded. "A *real* Long Tom!"

The ball bounced along the concrete toward the boy who had called himself "Winner Win." He picked it up and his eyes held an odd expression as he tossed the ball down the drive toward Steve. "Try another one. I'll bet you don't even hit the backboard, maybe not even the garage!"

Steve looked quickly at his challenger, then picked up the ball, again using but one hand. He hefted the sphere and eyed the basket.

Shucks, he thought, we had basketball and baskets up home. I never was real good, but I *have* made baskets before.

He took careful aim and let go. The high arc of the ball carried it above the backboard. It hit the louvered vent in the peak of the garage gable.

A loud, jeering laugh came from Winner Win. He glanced at Deadeye Dick and Fumbling Fred as though expecting them to join him. Neither boy laughed.

"Kind of 'pears like I was just lucky the first

time," Steve Reynolds said. His voice was soft and drawly, typically north Georgia. "Reckon y'all can't blame a feller for tryin', though."

The "can't" came out "kain't."

Fred grinned. "Come on and get in the game," he invited. "We're playing 21."

"Can't say I know how it's played."

"You take a long shot and a follow-in short shot. The long one has to be from at least twenty feet out. It counts two points if you make it. No more than two dribbles from where you get the rebound for the short shot. It goes as a one-pointer no matter how far you are from the basket when you shoot. The first guy who gets twenty-one points wins the game."

Fred smiled at Steve. "Haven't seen you around at school," Fred said. "You must be new in town."

"Couldn't be much newer, I reckon. Folks moved down here from Georgia two days back. I haven't been to school yet."

"I'm Fred Conley." The blond boy pointed to Dick Meredith and then at Winthrop Prouty and gave their names. "Win has an advantage over the rest of us," Fred said. "They had a regular basketball coach at the camp where he spent the summer."

"Yeah." Dick nodded. "Win won't let anybody forget that!"

"Pleasured to know y'all," the tall boy said. "I'm Steve Reynolds."

"Short for Steven?" Dick Meredith asked.

"No. I was named Steve, after my grand-daddy."

"What's your full name?"

"Steve Lund Reynolds."

"Steve Lunk Reynolds." Winthrop Prouty laughed nastily. "It figures!"

Steve was not quite sure how Prouty had said his middle name. "There has been a Steve in the Reynolds family for more than a hundred years," he said. "Lund was my mother's family name before she married Pa."

"Oh! I thought you said Steve *Lunk* Reynolds —and for sure that figures!"

Steve eyed Winthrop Prouty. "Y'all maybe think there is something wrong with my name?" Steve asked mildly.

"Of course, there is nothing wrong with it!" Fred Conley spoke hastily. He glared at Winthrop Prouty, saying "You're not funny!"

Dick Meredith's eyes sparkled as he looked at Steve. "Never heard Steve shortened," Dick said. "And I never heard of Lund as a name, period." Dick's brows drew together. "Has to be *something*, though!"

"There is this thing with Dick," Fred Conley explained. "He has to give everybody a nickname. Let's get started. You shoot first, Win, to set a good pattern. Then Steve will—"

"How's for calling him 'Stepladder'?" Prouty broke in on Fred. "You'd need a stepladder to get up where he—"

"Knock it off!" Dick Meredith interrupted Prouty. "I'll think of something. Go on and shoot at the basket instead of shooting off your mouth!"

Winthrop Prouty pushed a one-hander through the hoop. He dashed in and grabbed the ball as it dropped. He dribbled twice, pivoted and hooked a looping shot over his shoulder. It hit dead center.

"Three points," he said. "See if you can match that kind of pattern, Steve Lunker—'scuse! I mean *Stepladder*—Reynolds!"

Steve saw the glowering frown that Dick Meredith sent toward Prouty, Fred Conley's glare at the dark-haired youth. Steve said nothing, tried to concentrate on shooting.

But his first try slammed against the backboard two feet above the metal hoop. By the time his gangling stride carried him to the wide rebound, the ball was farther from the basket than his first try had been. His second effort fell far short.

"Well, I reckon a feller kain't help but say it 'pears like you-all lost your luck!"

Prouty's tone was an exaggerated mockery of Steve's drawl. Prouty looked toward Fred Conley and Dick Meredith as though he expected admiration.

"Will you knock it off!" Dick's scowl was deeper and blacker. "Everybody *couldn't* be as good as you!"

Fred nodded. "The chances are that Steve never had coaching from a big Princeton star the way you did!"

Winthrop Prouty gave every evidence that he had profited well from the summer camp coaching, at least in ability to shoot baskets. Rarely did he fail to make at least one of his tries for the basket. More often than not, he dropped both through the hoop. It took him exactly nine turns to score twenty-one points.

"Name of the game again, 21," he said when the final shot dropped into the basket. He looked at Steve. "Anybody would *need* a stepladder to get 'way up to your score! Seven, wasn't it?"

Steve nodded. He was well aware that he was being made fun of, but it did not particularly bother him.

"That's about as low as anybody ever ended up with." Prouty tossed the ball toward Steve. "You shoot first this game. You can get a head start."

"Reckon I would need a long head start to get near twenty-one 'fore you fellers."

"I can't play another game," Dick Meredith said. "Mom told me to get home in time to go to the store for her before noon."

"Store!" The word was a startled ejaculation

from Steve. He hastily dropped the ball. "Great day, I clean forgot! I clean forgot telling Fluorescence I wouldn't be gone long, too. Y'all have to excuse me. I got to hurry!"

Steve Lund Reynolds took off down the driveway.

CHAPTER TWO

A Pet, a Plan, and a Teacher

STEVE's long legs ate up the distance as he trotted homeward from the store. He came to the corner nearest the Reynolds residence. He looked one way before starting to cross the street. Then he looked in the opposite direction and was startled to meet the gaze of Fred Conley.

"Boy, when you said you had to hurry, you weren't just talking!" Fred pushed away from the utility pole he had been slouching against. "I bet I haven't been here two minutes. You went to the store, bought whatever you're carrying and got back in about the same time it took me to chuck the ball in the garage and hike over here."

Steve just stood looking at the other boy. "Of course," Fred said, "I did circle around and come through the alley. I didn't know which way you would be coming and I didn't want to miss you."

"Why?" Steve's tone held as much surprise as his expression. "I sure can't think why y'all would be anxious not to miss me."

"Couple of things you said: you told Fluorescence you wouldn't be long is one. That's a name I never heard before." Fred Conley grinned. "It would be fun to hear how Dick would make a nickname out of Fluorescence!"

Steve looked blank. Then he recalled that Fred had mentioned "this thing" about Dick Meredith and names. "I'd like to meet anybody with such an unusual name," Fred said. "Is Fluorescence a kid sister or brother?"

Steve glanced at Fred, then dropped his eyes. He moved uneasily. He said, "Fluorescence is not exactly a—a—well, Fluorescence is—is—doggone! There just is no sense in you waitin' here for me! I hope you won't take it wrong, but I just don't believe you had better meet Fluorescence. Can't you just forget the whole thing?"

"No, I kain't!" Fred grinned, instantly sobered and added, "Skip the supposed-to-be-humor. I really like to hear you say *can't*. Look, you know your own business, but believe me I don't want to meet your—whatever Fluorescence is, to laugh at her.

Fred studied the tall youth. "Maybe that stuff Prouty handed out bugged you," Fred said. "He kind of stole Dick's stuff and it did not set well with Dick. Don't mind any cruddy thing Prouty comes up with. It's hard to figure him, but he—well, let it go."

"I don't mind names. A feller gets used to them. Kids up in Georgia called me things worse than 'Lunk' or 'Stepladder.' "

Steve shrugged, as though all this was of small consequence to him. He said, "If y'all really want to meet up with Fluorescence, come on along."

They crossed the street and Fred said, "I don't get it. Fluorescence is a cute name for a dog or cat. How come you kind of got upset over me meeting— you did say her? Something wrong with Fluorescence?"

"No, just different." Steve turned into the cinder drive that led to the Reynolds garage. "I'll put this hamburger in the fridge and be right out."

Fred walked idly along the driveway. Suddenly he came to a stop as though frozen in his tracks, staring beyond the garage.

Steve came out of the house to find Fred still staring at a small animal with white markings straining at a leash fastened to the palm tree.

"So, now you know." Steve grinned. "Meet Fluorescence."

"She's a skunk!" Fred abruptly lost the immobility that held him. "A sure-enough skunk! Boy, oh-boy, oh-boy! It's a cinch Miss Smith won't have any part of you if you ever come to school smelling of Fluorescence! She had a bad enough time with Red Jeffery!"

Steve unfastened the leash and picked up his pet. Fluorescence was about the size of a small cat. Her fur was mostly glossy black. A white line on the forehead and a patch of white on her nape split into two stripes extending along her back. The head of the animal was small with a thick, blunt snout.

Fluorescence waved a bushy tail and nuzzled her nose against Steve's hand. He stroked her back.

"Y'all got no call to talk about Fluorescence stinking." He thrust the animal toward Fred. "Smell! She has no more odor than a cat and she is just as clean!"

Fred Conley backed away, but he realized as he did that there was no skunk odor about Fluorescence. The slight muskiness was inoffensive. "She *is* a skunk, though," he said. Then with questioning doubt: "Isn't she?"

"A representative of one of several branches of small carnivorous mammals of the weasel family." Steve nodded. He sounded as if he had memorized the words. "Mustedidae is the name for the big family. Fluorescence is of a sub-family, Mephitinae. Elongated toes with long, retractable claws and no webs are characteristic of this family. Mephitinae are notorious for large anal glands and the strong, highly offensive odor of the anal gland secretion. They simply turn their backs to any creature that disturbs them, raise their tails and fire away. They can eject fifteen to twenty feet."

Steve chuckled and his speech again became the relaxed drawl that fascinated Fred.

"That's straight from a reference book," Steve said. "Fluorescence *is* a skunk. Retractable means she can pull back her claws like a cat, and if Pa and a neighbor up in Georgia hadn't removed her anal gland when she was a kitten, Fluorescence could spray you with that horrible stinking stuff."

Steve stroked his pet again.

"But she can't spray and she is a better mouser, ratter and bug-beatle eater than any cat that ever lived. Besides being a swell guy to have around, aren't you, Fluorescence?"

The animal nuzzled her master's hand and her tail waved contentedly. There was defiance in Steve's attitude as he eyed Fred Conley.

"I don't know anything about Miss Smith or Red Jeffery but I have to tell you that nobody is making me get rid of Fluorescence!"

Fred Conley looked at the black-furred animal, nuzzling and sniffing and making a noise very near purring. "She is a mouser and ratter and eater of bugs and beatles," Fred mused. "And she sure goes for you. I'll buy Fluorescence, skunk or harmless kitty-cat from the wilds."

He eyed Steve.

"What I'm thinking about is not pets but a basketball team," Fred said. "And I'm also thinking that you are just what Samantha School needs."

"Samantha School?"

"That's the school you will be going to Monday. It's named after the first teacher who came into this area when it was considered part of the Everglades. Say, come to think of it, maybe Miss Smith is a descendant of that old gal whose picture hangs in the hall at school. The metal thing beneath the picture reads: *Pioneer Educator—Samantha Smith*."

Steve said, "And the deal Miss Smith had with Red Jeffery?"

"Well, Miss Smith is teacher of our room. She's swell. She wouldn't ever want to embarrass anybody. But heck, nobody could embarrass Red Jeffery! Red's father ran a trap line when he was a boy up in Wisconsin. So he wanted Red to set traps down here. Maybe there are as many furry animals here as up there, I don't know. But the only thing that ever got in one of Red's traps was a skunk— civet cat, they call it around here. But Red sure smelled like he tangled with a skunk!

"He came to school right from running the trap line and he sure did stink! Miss Smith stood it a while, then she sent Red home to take a bath and change clothes. She felt awful bad, but like I said, nobody could embarrass Red."

Fred stopped speaking. He was still eying Fluorescence warily. Steve put his pet on the ground and Fluorescence slithered across to Fred, sniffed at his feet, then rubbed against his leg as a cat might have done.

"She likes you!" Steve was amazed. "She never made friends so quick before!"

Fred backed away again, clearly not quite ready to accept the animal.

"What about this basketball team y'all plan?"

"Well, I had visions of being the big wheel," Fred said. "I've shot baskets and horsed around with Red Jeffery and Mike Whitney and Whitey Kemp, besides Win Prouty and Dick Meredith but it finally got through my thick head that this particular ball game is not something I could star at. So-o-o, I planned to get Miss Smith to sponsor a team officially and maybe I could sort of help run it."

Fred stopped, his eyes on Steve. The tall boy looked puzzled.

"You played that twenty-one game a lot better than I did," he said slowly. "But you're counting yourself out in this plan for a basketball team. Where do I come in?"

"Basketball is a tall guy's game. Look at the pro stars—Wilt Chamberlain, Bill Russell, Elgin Baylor —they were all big men. George Mikan was the big-name star from college basketball who pulled professional basketball along when it was getting started, and he was big-man as well as big-name. How about Lew Alcindor? The seven-foot-plus wonder is a cinch to eventually be right up there in the record books with other big men."

Steve had no idea what Fred was talking about. He had never before heard any of the names that rolled off Fred's tongue.

"Basketball is for tall guys," Fred repeated. "More and more a team goes nowhere without at least one big, tall guy to battle for rebounds off the backboards."

Fred's gaze traveled over Steve once more.

"You're big and tall," Fred said. "And you didn't show any more awkwardness than Dick or me —not as much as me—taking rebounds. 'Course, Win Prouty is smoother, he's had coaching. But you will get slicker with practice. We won't be playing games until after New Year's and that will give plenty of time to practice and get—"

Fred Conley broke off as though something had been abruptly stuffed in his mouth. He stared at two women who came around the corner of the garage.

The shorter woman was talking, looking up at the other. "I am sure you will find working with the Mothers' Club a worthwhile and gratifying experience, Mrs. Reynolds."

Then she saw the boys and called, "Why, hello, Fred!"

Fred swallowed. Steve wondered if Fred had any idea of the consternation in his tone as he gulped and answered, "Hello, Miss Smith!"

CHAPTER THREE

Mom and Dad Think Differently

Miss Smith stared wide-eyed at Fluorescence.

Fred Conley looked from Miss Smith to the lady beside her. This had to be Steve's mother. Her hair was the same shade of brown, her eyes were the same soft gray, and she was tall for a woman. Mrs. Reynolds gave him a friendly smile, then looked at her son.

"He's Fred Conley, Mom," Steve said. "He lives in the next block toward town."

"How nice that you have found a friend so soon!" Mrs. Reynolds beamed. "Miss Smith," she said, "my son, Steve."

"Hello, Steve." Miss Smith transferred her gaze

briefly from Fluorescence to the tall boy. "Welcome to our community." She smiled tentatively at Steve's pet but almost imperceptibly fell back a step.

"Fluorescence is not a skunk like the one Red Jeffery tangled with, Miss Smith!" The words tumbled from Steve. "She can't—that is, Fluorescence does not have the—what I mean is—" He looked at his mother and said in a tone of desperation, "Tell her about Fluorescence, Mom!"

Mrs. Reynolds raised her eyebrows, clearly surprised. Then she inclined her head as though she suddenly saw a light.

"It never occurs to me that anybody should wonder about Fluorescence, Miss Smith," she said. "Three or four years ago when Steve's father prepared a new field for cultivation, he plowed out a family of skunks. There were four young left but the mother was killed by the plow. Neighbors took three of the kittens and we kept one for Steve. They all had their scent glands removed and as far as I am concerned, Fluorescence has been a blessing.

"She keeps my flower borders and my garden free of insects. We have never seen a mouse since she has been with us. Whatever experience you had with somebody else's animal, you need have no worry about Fluorescence."

Miss Smith was eying Fred Conley. Fred squirmed. "She was a shock to me, too," he said. "I— I—I just blurted out about you sending Red home!"

Steve really saw Miss Smith as she stood looking at Fluorescence. She was a full head shorter than
his mother. Her hair was the exact color of fields of
ripe buckwheat that Pa had raised many times. Her
eyes were blue and there were fine lines around the
corners that gave evidence she smiled a lot.

"I came to visit new members of our little community as an unofficial welcoming committee of
one," she said. "But it seems that one never loses the
identity of a teacher."

She looked at Steve, then at Fluorescence and
smiled slightly. "I would suggest," Miss Smith said,
"that Fluorescence—and how appropriate that
name sounds!—be a pet at home, without public-
ity." She glanced from Steve to the other boy. "Don't
you agree, Fred?"

"Yes, ma'am. Oh, yes, ma'am, I agree!"

Steve saw from the start that there was a definite division among the boys Fred Conley brought
together to make up a basketball team.

Red Jeffery, Dick Meredith and Mike Whitney
were with Fred. But Win Prouty's attitude had not
changed. He plainly resented Fred's friendliness toward Steve. A very blond boy called Whitey Kemp,
husky Jerry Freed, and a quiet boy named Bill Alton
quite evidently went along with Winthrop Prouty.

"Just because he's a stepladder-tall freak does

not make him a basketball player!" Prouty protested when Fred said he thought that Steve should be center. "I played center for our camp team. A center has to be a good ball-handler and passer, clever at setting up plays and a good shot. This guy is clumsy and awkward handling the ball and he can't shoot. He has never played basketball!"

"None of us has played basketball with a regular team, except you. All of us—excepting you again —will be clumsy at ball-handling and stuff. That's why we have to find out who is going to play where and then practice as a team."

"Look who knows so much! What position do you figure on playing?"

Fred flushed and dropped his eyes at Prouty's question. Steve moved uneasily. Then Fred raised his gaze and faced Prouty squarely.

"I'm not figuring on playing any position," Fred said. "As far as knowing so much, there are *some* things you don't know as well as coaches of big college and pro teams!"

Now it was Prouty who flushed angrily. "Who put you in the class of college and pro coaches?" he blustered. "You been made coach of this team, or something?"

"Knock it off!" Dick Meredith gave Prouty a disgusted look. "For sure we are not going to get any practice listening to you blow off!"

"Yeah, let's get with it! . . . Who cares who

gives out with info? . . . Well, Prouty played under a real coach on a regular team!"

"I haven't been made a coach." Fred continued to look steadily at Prouty. "But I haven't heard that you have been made a coach, either. Miss Smith is all for us getting up a basketball team. She will arrange some games with other teams later. Right now, she is on a committee planning things for the junior high school we will have next year. She *suggested* that I could sort of get things organized."

"And another suggestion right now would be to get started!" Red Jeffery glared at Prouty, then shifted his eyes to Fred. "Nobody is going to say today that so-and-so will play such-and-such and that is it! Fred, take charge and run us through whatever stuff you think we should do!"

A silence held after Red Jeffery's words. He and Dick Meredith and Mike Whitney moved a little toward Fred. Whitey Kemp, Jerry Freed and Bill Alton looked toward Prouty. Winthrop Prouty hesitated, then shrugged.

"Okay, so get things organized," he said.

Fred gave a quick glance at Prouty, then said, "Basketball is a game of who-controls-the-backboards, who-gets-the-rebounds. That comes from a college coach who has taken ten teams to national tournaments in the past twelve years. So let's start with practice at grabbing rebounds."

Fred tossed the ball against the backboard. The

boys broke into groups of three. "One is the shooter," Fred said. "The book says that a shooter should always follow-in his shot. One of the other two is a teammate of the shooter, the third is a defensive man. The guy who gets the rebound scores a rebound—and don't ever think the count of snagging rebounds isn't kept as being about as important as field goals!"

Steve had no great enthusiasm as practice began. But soon he was right in the middle of the competition, surprised that he got more rebounds than others. Some of the boys he defeated began to sputter.

"How are you going to have a chance at the ball when a big ox like him jumps up there? . . . What's a guy supposed to do, mow him down to get at the ball? That's a foul! . . . I had that one figured and was waiting, so what happens? That oversized lummox reached right over me and glommed the ball! . . . You need a stepladder to get to the big hippo!"

At the end of practice Steve felt good.

He felt good after the second practice session. He had grabbed more rebounds than any other boy. He felt especial satisfaction from having taken the ball away from Winthrop Prouty in five of six personal encounters.

The third day of practice, Prouty said, "There is more to this game than taking rebounds off the backboards—and I don't care what some Mr. Big wrote in a book! You have to make baskets to mark up scores. That's the main idea—to score. I say we should have more practice at shooting baskets!"

"I'll go along with that! . . . Yeah! . . . No good getting the ball if you don't make some baskets!" The other boys agreed enthusiastically.

Steve was acutely aware that in the basket shooting department he was lowest. Fred Conley walked from practice with the big boy.

"Y'all stick your neck out for me all the time," Steve said. "That Prouty feller is right in saying I can't shoot. I'm as awkward as he says, too."

"That'll be enough talk like that!" Fred spoke sharply. "Get it through your head that you can make our team a good team or just a gang putting out a poor effort. So you have a lot to learn, we all do. It could be that I can help."

Shortly before they reached the Conley drive Steve made up his mind. He was going to tell Fred that while he was helping a big, clumsy guy from Georgia, he was losing out with longtime friends and Winthrop Prouty. Steve drew in a breath and was ready to talk when the other boy spoke.

"Don't be discouraged. A team that has a big man has the edge—and for sure there are no kid teams around here that have guys bigger than you! Stay in there and hang tough and pay no attention to Prouty!"

"It boils down to where I am a kind of millstone around Fred's neck." Steve looked at his parents. Mom knew Fred from the day that Miss Smith had called on her. Pa was a quiet man who rarely took issue with anybody, especially Mom, and seemed really interested only when his work was the topic. But Pa was solid. Steve said, "What about it, Pa?"

"You feel that you are causing this Fred Conley a lot of grief, son?"

"Yes, sir. Fred is a real friend. He knows about Fluorescence and has never said a word about her. Fred is the kind of friend that a fellow just can't see put in a bad spot, if he can help.

"Basketball is a big thing with Fred. I am not a good basketball player, but there is a good player named Winthrop Prouty. It may be that he could do a better job at getting up a team than Fred because he has played on a regular team with a regular coach. Fred sticks up for me and takes grief from Prouty and other kids. I am going to quit the basketball team. I don't want Fred to have a rough time just because of me."

"One minute," Steve's father said. "It's best to consider all sides before jumping to a decision."

Mr. Reynolds was not a small man, but he was shorter than his son by an inch or so and a little stooped as though he bent over a lot. His hands were not unclean but they were roughened by outdoor work, as were his nails.

"Let's consider some things." Mr. Reynolds inclined his head. "Such as why I gave up a job in Georgia that paid more than I am earning here."

Mrs. Reynolds looked at her husband. She said, "George, would you like me to remind Steve why we left Georgia?"

"I would like you to just keep quiet for a moment." There was no sharpness or anger in George Reynolds' words. But there was also no room for doubt that he wanted no interference. He eyed his son.

"There is nothing wrong with the north Georgia hill country," he said. "My pappy and his pappy and his pappy as far back as you want, raised families there. Nobody ever went hungry. We could have stayed in the hill country and done all right.

"We came down here when an opportunity to do the work that I like best was offered, but that alone would never have caused me to leave north Georgia. The big reason was that you would be provided with a new environment—and have a better chance to grow in more than one way."

Mr. Reynolds glanced at Mrs. Reynolds and smiled. "That came from your mother, a Yankee-trained schoolmarm," he went on. "Now, would you upset all your mother's plans?"

George Reynolds eyed his son and his wife, and Steve was sure that he saw a twinkle in his father's eyes.

"I am only a gardener, working for a monthly wage," Mr. Reynolds said. "Mr. Grundy has all the fine equipment a man needs to rightly tend lawns and gardens, and I don't mind going a mile or so to get to his place.

"There are also possibilities of one day developing my own caretaking business and—but I'm wandering away from the main idea. We are here, and we are going to BE here. You have made a friend. From what you and your mother say, Fred Conley is a fine boy. You cannot abandon him and just quit this basketball team. You would be letting your friend down."

George Reynolds glanced briefly at his wife, then went on. "Your mother and I think entirely different from you in the matter of dropping out of basketball. You owe it to Fred to stick with it, and we want you to do so."

CHAPTER FOUR

Practices

STEVE began to wonder who was letting whom down.

Fred Conley made no effort to engage in the practice sessions, physically. But it seemed to Steve that Fred had eyes in the back and both sides of his head.

"There is a difference between offensive rebounding and defensive rebounding, Steve! . . . Try to keep between your man and the basket on defense, but if you can't, GET UP THERE AFTER HE SHOOTS! . . . Use your height! . . . Judge where the rebound is going!"

At times Steve thought that Fred watched nobody but him. Then Fred would come up with something aimed at Dick Meredith or Red Jeffery. Sometimes he would yell at Mike Whitney or Whitey Kemp or Jerry Freed or Bill Alton. But Fred never shouted at Win Prouty.

After the fourth practice, Steve said half-jokingly to Fred on the way home, "Y'all sure was on me. Most of the time. Why don't you ever tell Prouty anything?"

"Well, I guess there are two reasons." Fred was very serious. "Prouty has been exposed to coaching from a real coach. All I know about basketball, really, is what I read and what I get from watching games on television."

Fred drew in a breath. "You just don't know what an addition you are," he said. "We have been thinking of something to sort of dramatize Samantha School—that is Miss Smith's term. I figure if we get a basketball team that can play one of the Beach City outfits and knock them off—or even give them a good game—we would be accepted."

Fred shrugged, then went on. "I'm at a big disadvantage," he said. "Things I pass on at practices are right out of a book. I couldn't do any of them. But if I can get you guys to do them well enough, we will make it really rough for teams that Miss Smith gets to play us!"

Steve waited, but when Fred did not continue, he asked, "What's the other reason?"

"Well, it's kind of wound up with the first. I don't think Prouty is naturally mean, he is more spoiled than anything. What Win thinks of me doesn't really matter. We need him on the team! So, a guy named Fred Conley is not going to risk making him get sore and quit the team!"

Fred stopped and scowled. "That makes me kind of chicken, I guess. If I was a real coach and—and—well, I'm not!"

"And you aren't going to risk Prouty maybe taking two or three other guys with him." Steve nodded. "I wouldn't say you're chicken. You're just playing things smart. So, a big character who never thought he was a basketball player had better sing kind of low!"

Practice went on. Prouty and his followers began to talk more and more about practicing as a team instead of drills and drills on individual play. Steve sympathized. But he knew that even though they seemed like drudgery, the drills were helping to overcome his awkwardness.

His confidence increased and he began to think of practice with the whole group as more than something that might make others laugh at him. For the first time he could remember, the fact that he was taller and bigger than other boys was not something to regret. Instead it was something to be proud of.

Then he became aware that the feeling between the followers of Winthrop Prouty and the guys who were with Fred Conley was increasingly bad. Steve got Dick Meredith aside after the fifth practice.

"Y'all maybe will laugh," Steve said, "but the way it looks to me, this Prouty feller and Fred are in a battle. Prouty has had honest-to-gosh coaching and he really is good. Okay.

"I don't want anything to happen that will hurt Fred. He absorbs everything he reads, I reckon. Stuff from coaches who have to be bigger in this basketball thing than anybody who coached at a summer camp for boys. So who is going to come out on top in this battle?"

Dick Meredith looked at him. A peculiar expression was in his eyes as he said, "How about that? Here I have been figuring you for an easy-going character who happened to have size, a guy Fred latched onto because Fred Conley latches onto anyone he thinks is an underdog.

"Okay," he went on. "I suppose I knew from the day we played 21 that Prouty would give you a bad time, if he could. Fred must have known it, too, and he took your side right then. I know I did.

"Prouty has more on the ball—basketball, that is!—than any of us, but Fred is beating his brains out and absorbing everything he reads and everything he hears or sees on TV about basketball."

Dick Meredith stopped. He looked up at Steve.

"Fred is convinced that basketball is a game for the big guy. So am I. You are our big guy. If you fall flat on your face, Fred and us guys who string along with him are going to fall just as flat! Fred *has* to come out on top against Prouty, or we're cooked as a basketball team! So get the message."

Before school was dismissed Friday, Miss Smith told the boys they would not be able to use the playground basketball court for practice.

"A general meeting of teachers and custodians has been called for 4:00 P.M. in town," she explained. "There is a rule that playground gates must be closed when no teacher or custodian is around the school. As you all know I am sure, school will not be in session again until Wednesday of next week."

Fred Conley and Steve left together at the end of the school day.

"The book I am studying now is HOW TO PLAY BETTER BASKETBALL," Fred said. "It outlines the how-to-do-it for basketball fundamentals. The chapter on 'Shooting Baskets' has something to say about every kind of shot there is, I guess."

Steve did not answer. He was thinking that he was just as well pleased there would be no basketball practice for a while. He had been neglecting Fluorescence.

"Are you hearing what I'm saying?" Fred asked.

"I'm hearing. But—but—well, I just don't have the enthusiasm for basketball that you have. I'd rather spend some time with Fluorescence than practice all the time."

Steve saw that Fred was hurt. He continued hastily, "But I want to do anything I can to help your basketball team!"

"It is NOT *my* basketball team! I keep telling you that—that—oh, nuts! Listen, will you?"

"Don't get all riled up. I'm listening."

"Okay. Making baskets started with a two-handed underhand shot and worked up to a two-handed shove shot from the chest. Then somebody found he could hit the basket better by holding the ball near his lips and flipping it with wrist and arm movement rather than a pushing motion. They called this a kiss shot.

"There weren't so many big guys then as there are today, but there were some. The bigger boys started raising the ball above their heads to keep it out of reach of the smaller guys. Somebody found he could fire from there with a two-handed overhead shot and it was tougher to guard."

They came to Fred's house.

"Your mom won't be expecting you early," Fred said. "You're a big guy. You ought to get that overhead shot down pat."

They practiced the overhead shot at the garage basket. Steve felt very uncomfortable holding the ball high while Fred jumped and batted vainly at the sphere.

"Don't just stand there holding it," Fred cried. "Shoot!"

Steve threw the ball. It did not come anywhere near the basket. As the sphere banged against the backboard, Steve ran in, left his feet and came down clutching the ball.

"Well, how about that!" Fred's tone held exultation. "The way to go! You rammed in there and grabbed the rebound! Try the overhead again."

"I feel kind of like I'm cheating," Steve said. "Holding the ball 'way up where you don't have a chance to get it!"

"Cut it out! You're big and tall, so use your weight and height. There is nothing unfair about it!"

Steve threw more than a hundred overhead shots before he began to feel less awkward. After a time the ball fell into the metal circle more often. The misses were by narrower margins.

"When you get so you can hit with the overhead and sink hook shots, you are going to show some Beach City kids a thing or two! You will be really tough to guard." Fred stopped and looked thoughtful. "But it will take a lot of practice," he went on after a moment. "You know something? I've got another ball. It's scuffed and kind of beat-up,

but it is still round. You could even make a mark on the back of your garage and fire hook shots and overheads at that.

"Talk it over with your mom and dad, huh?"

Steve was well aware that neither his mother or father knew much about basketball. There would be little use in talking things over with Mom or Pa.

On the other hand, though Fluorescence did not know anything about basketball either, she was a mighty good listener. A fellow could pour out his innermost thoughts to her and she would only switch her tail back and forth and maybe purr. So Steve held his pet and talked to her as though she were human.

"I reckon we've come to a place where we have to put out some extra effort," he said. "Now, y'all know I am naturally lazy, Fluorescence. All this practice and practice and practice that Fred talks about—y'all know it's nothing I want to do.

"Then you have to look at something else—this Winthrop Prouty feller. That first day when he called himself Winner Win, I reckon he was not funnin' like Dick and Fred when they called themselves other names. Right off, Prouty didn't like me and I didn't like him. We don't like him any better now because he could throw a big fat block against the thing that Fred wants most, you see."

Steve silently stroked the fur of his pet before he went on.

"Fred tried to make things clear to me. Fred is just too nice a feller to lay everything out on the line, but Dick Meredith did. Fred took my side and Dick is with him. So is Red Jeffery and a couple of other kids. But it looks as though a tall feller from Georgia is going to be right in there either winning for Fred or losing."

He scratched a big hand along the backbone of Fluorescence. His eyes were somber. One of his oversized feet kicked out and slammed a clump of dirt against the palm tree behind the garage.

"All right!" There was a finality in Steve's tone. "We'll get us a basket put up, Fluorescence. Pa will help when he understands the situation. We'll fasten it back here on the garage and I'll practice and practice and practice. Whatever Fred has me do at regular team sessions, I'll work on it more here. Maybe 'Stepladder Steve' can get good enough to help Fred come out on top against 'Winner Win' Prouty!"

CHAPTER FIVE

Fluorescence Does Not Agree

MR. REYNOLDS was absorbed in a catalog of shrubbery, plants and flower seeds. Mrs. Reynolds sat in an old-fashioned rocker, knitting. Steve casually approached the television set in front of them. He said, "Anything either of you particularly want on TV?"

"I'm not really watching." Mrs. Reynolds smiled. "If there is something you want to see, just switch channels."

Steve said, "You, Pa?"

Mr. Reynolds did not look up from the catalog.

"George!" Mrs. Reynolds spoke her husband's name with some sharpness. He looked at her inquiringly. "Do you mind if Steve changes channels?"

"To me it is mostly only noise." Mr. Reynolds shrugged. "Tune in whatever you want."

Steve turned the selector dial. A roaring noise came before the picture, and a voice said, "The crowd appreciates that once again Big Bob has shown his value to a team. Not only did he clog up the middle lane to keep the Lakers from working in for a close-in shot, he batted the ball away an instant after it left Waltham's hand. Then he literally took the ball away from Waltham when it seemed that Waltham would regain possession. Speaking from experience, I can testify that when you take a ball away from the Lakers' super-star, you have done something!"

Mr. Reynolds was absorbed again in his seed catalog. Mrs. Reynolds glanced at the screen when the picture came on, watched for a moment while five tall men in white uniforms passed a basketball, faked passes, dribbled, tried every way they knew to get one of their players free of dark-clad opponents for a shot at the basket. She smiled at Steve and he knew it was purely mechanical. Mom had no more interest in basketball than Pa, and neither one of them knew anything about the sport.

The televised professional game went on. A player in dark uniform leaped in front of a white-clad man and intercepted a pass. He dribbled away fast, then fired the ball to a teammate and cut for the foul lane. He took a return flip. The sphere had scarcely touched his hand before the big Los Angeles Laker pushed a one-handed shot toward the basket. The ball hit the rim and bounced. The shooter leaped high and tapped it through the ring.

"And there is the greatness of Gaylord Waltham in a capsule!" The announcer's words were drowned by the crowd noise. When it died out somewhat, he said, "I had the privilege—privilege, heck, the *task!*—of being assigned to guard Gaylord Waltham during his rookie season. He was good then; he is better now. He has all the moves, instinctive reactions, size and speed. The big men in basketball today are more than merely big. They are agile. They are clever. They keep the pressure constantly on the other guy.

"Basketball is increasingly a big man's game. Big Bob is a standout for the Celtics, Gaylord Waltham for the Lakers, Brute Smith for the Warriors and—well, go over the rosters of pro teams and you will see that big men control the game!"

Steve watched the smooth play of the professionals. He asked himself a question: I wonder if those big guys were ever as awkward and clumsy as I am?

A basket was made by another player in Laker uniform and a third Laker stole the ball shortly after the Celtics passed in from out of bounds. A fast break notched another field goal for the visiting team. The Boston Celtics called time out. The announcer answered Steve's mental question almost as though he had heard it.

"We had Big Bob and Waltham on a half-time program the last time the Celtics visited L.A. I was never classed as a BIG man in the NBA, but I was bigger than other kids my age, and I was curious to know whether other oversize boys had gone through any of the agony I did in growing up.

"So, I asked Big Bob and Gaylord Waltham if they were always as smooth and coordinated and clever—and both broke into the question with loud laughter before I finished it. Listen to this tape of some things they said."

"Smooth and clever and coordinated, he asks!" Big Bob chuckled. "Man, I used to sneak down back streets and duck and hide so other kids couldn't get me into some game and laugh at what a clumsy ox I was!"

"Welcome to the club," Waltham said. "Nobody could *really* have been in the same SAD club I belonged to. SAD stands for Stupid Awkward Donkey! You maybe think you had things rough because you were bigger than other kids but let me tell you—"

An announcer broke into the tape recording of the two stars' comments. The sportscaster came back on the air after a commercial.

"Big Bob and Gaylord Waltham agreed—and I

certainly go along with them—that a fellow is not automatically a basketball player because nature made him big and tall. You practice and you practice and you practice. You get to realize that becoming adept at basketball is your best bet to pull even with the smaller, sharper guys.

"Waltham says he started with a beat-up ball that he finally had to stuff because the cover wore through and it wouldn't hold air. But he kept throwing the thing at a barrel hoop he fastened to the woodshed behind a plantation cabin down in Alabama. Big Bob had the advantage of playground basketball courts in his city, but he emphatically states that practice and work and work and practice are the ingredients by which big boys become proficient at basketball—or boys of any size, for that matter."

Steve frowned. The action began again on the TV screen, but he was no longer interested. He started from the room.

His mother asked, "Anything I can get you, Steve?"

"Never mind, Mom. I just remembered something I was going to do." Steve grinned. "For once it is not a trip to the fridge!"

Steve rummaged in a jumbled pile in the back of the garage. He thought he had seen something there the other day that would be useful now. Fluorescence was with him, sniffing and poking her nose beneath things and in corners, carrying on a never-ending search for insects or mice or anything she could gobble.

"Doggone, Fluorescence," Steve said. "Maybe it was before we moved, but somewhere I saw a riggin' that would make a swell basket to fasten to the garage."

He unpiled various articles. Then he saw a piece of metal that was bent in round shape and started to pull at it. A quiet drawl came from behind him.

" 'Pears like if a man is going to have any peace, he has to do something not rightly clear but somehow will help his young'un." George Reynolds surveyed his son.

"I told Mom to never mind," Steve said.

"That was a long way from being enough." Steve's father spoke dryly. "Your ma is purely persistent! What in time are you looking for?"

Steve explained without going into detail that Fred Conley wanted him to practice basketball. "This thing I'm trying to pull loose might be about the size of a regular basket," he finished.

He did not notice his father's peculiar look as Mr. Reynolds moved a box of miscellaneous bolts and screws. Then he pried some long boards off the metal ring and Steve easily pulled it free. The boy frowned and muttered, "This *is* a basket, Pa. Where the heck did it come from?"

"So that *was* what the boss meant." George Reynolds chuckled. "Must have been something in the back of my mind kept me from carting it off to the dump. It purely does not look like any basket I ever saw, though!"

"Pa!" Steve looked at his father. "You kidding me? You must have seen baskets in games on TV!"

"Like I told your ma, television is mostly background noise. I hardly ever look at it, less'n it's one of the shows your ma and me like—and basketball is not one of those shows."

Mr. Reynolds chuckled.

"I've seen young'uns tossing balls at hoops fastened to garages and barns and such," he said. "And I suppose you could call me dumb for not knowing they was baskets—but a hoop, a simple ring does not 'pear to me to deserve being called a basket. I was kind of stumped when Mr. Grundy told me to take the basket his grandson had used off the garage."

His son explained.

"They hang netting from the rim in gymnasiums and playground basketball courts. Fred Conley read that the man who invented basketball first used peach baskets for goals. But the ball stayed in when a goal was made, so they cut the bottom out. Then the wooden baskets didn't last long, so they put up metal rings with nets, but they were still called baskets. Anyway, this is an honest-to-gosh basket, braces and all. Can I fasten it to the back of the garage?"

"I'll help you put it up."

Steve dribbled the basketball around while his father measured to get the basket the proper ten feet up from the ground and began drilling holes. Mr. Reynolds called Steve to hold the framework in place while he tightened the bolts from inside. Steve rolled the ball toward his pet.

The skunk's short legs pistoned as she whirled around and chased the ball. Steve watched her play with it while he stood on the ladder holding the braces in place. Fluorescence jabbed a front paw at the ball. It moved and she jumped back. Then she crouched and sprang at the ball much as a cat would play with it. Only the basketball was much bigger than Fluorescence. She would leap at it, jab the scuffed leather, then bound back and leap again.

"Dribble it!" Steve called. "Get your nose under it and shoot a basket!"

It seemed as though Fluorescence understood him. She poked her nose under the ball and lifted her head. The ball rolled farther than she had been able to move it with her paw. Her leaps and footwork in making swift turns amused Steve. If I could move the way she does, he thought, I would have this basketball business made!

The bolts were finally tightened and the basket was ready for use. Steve began dribbling, shooting, following in for rebounds. His pet entered heartily into this new game her master was playing. Whenever Steve missed a rebound and the ball bounced and rolled on the ground, Fluorescence ran beside him making darting movements toward the ball as he dribbled. Several times Steve narrowly missed falling over her.

Then came a time when he was unable to avoid his pet. He swerved and tried to leap aside but one foot thumped into the animal. Steve was thrown off stride. The heel of one foot caught the canvas at the arch of his other basketball shoe.

Steve sprawled. The ball rolled away and Fluorescence chased after it while Steve stared in dismay at his shoe. About four inches of sole was ripped loose from the canvas top. He took off the shoe. Maybe Mom could sew it together. Steve squatted and called his pet.

"Okay, girl, you have had it! Come here!" Fluorescence came unsuspectingly. "I can't get in much practice mostly dodging you," Steve said. "Back on the leash you go!"

Fluorescence switched her bushy tail. Her head

shook from side to side as though she was expressing strong disagreement.

"Okay, so you are a dissenter," Steve said. "Stage a protest march, it will get you nowhere. This way it will be safer for both of us—and easier on my shoes!"

CHAPTER SIX

Two Surprises

No SCHOOL today, no school tomorrow. How about if they had conferences for teachers Monday and Tuesday of every week?

Steve considered. A lot of kids might cheer and yell, but would they really mean it? For sure a fellow named Steve Reynolds would not cheer. He liked going to Samantha School. He liked Miss Smith. The kids in sixth grade were all swell and— well, maybe not quite *all!*

"What do you say, Steve?"

Steve looked around. The question came from Fred Conley as he turned the corner of the garage. Fred flipped a hand in greeting then he took in the steel rim fastened to the back of the garage and his eyes widened. "Something new has been added!" he cried.

Steve tried to be nonchalant. He told Fred how his father had saved the honest-to-goodness basket after removing it from the back of Mr. Grundy's garage.

"Why didn't I think of that basket!" Fred smote his forehead with the butt of his hand. "Mr. Grundy would have let us come up there and use the basket, but I never thought a thing about it still being there.

"Lots of people around here think Mr. Grundy is a sour-puss," Fred went on. "He's not, I like him a lot. He was nuts about his grandson and when he said he needed a basket for practice, Mr. Grundy ordered one from Beach City. Mr. Grundy didn't know from nothing about basketball, but he had the sport shop send a man to install the basket the right height and everything. Well, anyway, things end up so you have a real basket for practice. What are we waiting for?"

Steve grinned at Fred. He was glad his friend had come. Fred said, "Put on your basketball shoes."

"Why?"

"Because you'll wear them in a game and we are going to practice pivoting and stopping and quick turns. You need to get the feel of regular basketball shoes while you do the footwork."

Steve brought his shoes and looked dubiously at his unevenly spaced stitching that held together the sole and canvas top of one of the shoes.

"Pretty crummy job." He talked to himself as much as he talked to Fred. "Mom could probably have fixed them a lot better, but she was busy at a Mothers' Club thing."

He gave the shoes critical inspection.

"I'd say that this torn one might last. But I have a feeling that the one really ripped from the canvas won't hold together very long."

"Can't tell until you try it," Fred said. "This famous coach who wrote the stuff on pivoting and spinning said that being able to pivot around an opponent without fouling is tough, but the really good offensive man must develop an ability to pivot and spin. According to him, a pivot is a definite stop, bending at the knees, anchoring one foot and moving the other leg right or left, depending on whether you are making a front pivot or reverse. A spin is a more continuous movement of the body without a definite stop, but both spin and pivot are similar. Try a pivot."

Steve frowned as he went over Fred's words in his mind. He lumbered forward a few steps, socked one foot down hard—and almost tripped himself when he swung the other foot across in front.

"Not bad," Fred said. "It's bound to seem kind of awkward at first. Try it again."

Steve tried again. He did not make a good pivot but he did not stumble or trip himself. He kept trying the move under Fred's coaching. *Fred may not be able to do the things he reads about,* Steve thought. *But he sure knows how they should be done! Too bad he can't do them.*

The twenty-first time proved that Steve's feeling about the ripped shoe was far too correct.

He threw his weight on the foot encased in the bad shoe and the strain was too great. The stitching gave way and Steve was abruptly sitting on the ground. The sole of his shoe dangled loosely from the canvas and his bare foot stuck out. Steve stared ruefully, then took off the wrecked shoe. He looked at the other one and began unlacing it.

"One is no good," he said.

"We might as well try a few more pivots," Fred said. "You're getting onto the technique. Maybe you can pivot better barefoot."

"Maybe." Steve shrugged. "That's the way I'll probably be playing from now on—barefoot."

"What do you mean?"

"Pa and Mom are saving, trying to get money ahead so that Pa can buy equipment to start his own landscaping and caretaking business. There is no money to buy me new basketball shoes."

"Write a letter to Santa Claus to bring you a pair for Christmas."

"I couldn't do that. Pa and Mom would cut

themselves short to get 'em. Just looks as though I will have to forget the basketball stuff."

"Hey, you can't do that!"

"Well, I can go on practicing now without shoes, anyway."

Oddly, Steve made better pivots after discarding the shoes. "Chances are you just got the hang of pivoting," Fred said. "As far as I know, there is no rule that a guy *has* to wear shoes. For sure, kids have played barefoot on our outdoor court. But I can just hear those Beach City kids yelling and jeering if you went out on their swell gymnasium floor with bare feet! Maybe there will be a Santa Claus *before* Christmas."

Steve gave no thought to Fred's remark. He was not surprised when his friend showed up again Tuesday, but he *was* surprised when Fred tore the newspaper wrapping from a bundle he carried and thrust a pair of basketball shoes at him.

"I told you there might be a Santa Claus before Christmas," Fred said.

Steve stared at the shoes. He made no move to take them.

Fred said, "They're yours. They are a gift from Mr. Grundy. See if they fit."

The tall boy flashed a look at Fred, then took the shoes. He put them on and laced them. They felt comfortable.

"Fit like they were made for me," Steve drawled. "Now, let's put some things together. There has to be more than a-gift-from-Mr.-Grundy. Y'all can't just hand out something like that!"

"Kain't we?" Fred grinned. "Sorry. That Georgia accent gets me."

"Give with the whole thing, you hear?"

"I told you that Mr. Grundy was nuts about his grandson," Fred said. "I remembered that he bought basketball shoes for young Grundy three or four years ago. His grandson wore them a few times but they were too big, or something. Anyway, he got another pair and these couldn't be returned because he had scuffed them."

Fred chuckled. "Mr. Grundy has plenty of money, but he said, quote: 'No use in things going to waste.' He gave the shoes to you when I told him about how you ruined yours, and he was really glad some use would be made of them."

Steve's expression still mirrored disbelief.

Fred went on. "He said something that I didn't understand. It was—'give 'em to him in appreciation of our rose garden being free of pests.' Does that mean anything to you?"

"Sure does!" Steve laughed. "And what it means is more of a surprise than Mr. Grundy giving me the shoes!"

Steve thought about Mr. Grundy's "free of pests" reference all the while Fred guided him through a long pivoting and spinning practice after he put on the basketball shoes. He beat Fred soundly in a game of 21 after the practice, but Steve was still thinking about Mr. Grundy.

He now had an excuse to go see him, thank him for the shoes. But mostly he wanted to make sure of what he already knew in his mind—Pa must have been taking Fluorescence with him over to Mr. Grundy's.

CHAPTER SEVEN

First Real Game

STEVE wondered why anyone would think Mr. Grundy was a sour-puss. His hair was white, but his face was tanned and unwrinkled. His brown eyes widened below bushy brows and then twinkled as he smiled up at Steve.

"You *are* a big one," Mr. Grundy said. "You're bigger than your dad, and I have to look up to him! What can I do for you—Steve, isn't it?"

"Mostly I came to thank you for the basketball shoes, sir. They're swell!"

"You are very welcome. Didn't young Conley tell you they are really an offering of appreciation?"

"Yes, sir. That's another reason I came. Pa has

been bringing my pet here, hasn't he? And you don't mind?"

"Of course I don't mind!" Mr. Grundy endeared himself forever in Steve's view when he added, "Fluorescence and I are friends. When I was a boy I had a pet squirrel, a pet gopher and a pet groundhog. I would have had a pet skunk, I suppose, if one had turned up. Fluorescence is a treasure!"

Mr. Grundy chuckled.

"Young Conley told me how she caused you to rip the sole of your basketball shoe from the top," he went on. "I'd like to see her dribble a basketball with her nose!"

"Dribble?" Steve gave the elderly gentleman a surprised look. "Fred said you didn't even know what a basket was!"

"So I didn't when my grandson talked me into having one installed at the back of the garage a half-dozen years ago. You might say that I learned about basketball in self-defense. You see, my grandson was —and is—a basketball nut! He is in college now and I seldom see him. But—come in a moment, Steve."

Steve followed Mr. Grundy into a long room at the back of the house. They stood before a large picture window and Mr. Grundy said, "I spend a considerable time here in late afternoon. I suppose I am indulging nostalgic memories of my grandson when he was about the age of you boys. The fact remains that I am more than casually interested in basketball."

Steve looked out the window. From it Mr. Grundy had an excellent view of the outdoor basketball court behind Samantha School.

"I have been watching Fred Conley trying to get you boys to do things—apparently from what he has read," Mr. Grundy said, "as he doesn't do them himself. By watching you I have acquired quite an interest in the basketball team that is going to represent Samantha School."

"Well, what do you know!" Steve marveled. "We didn't realize that anybody watched us."

Again Mr. Grundy chuckled. "I had to have your dad remove two palm trees to get a clear view," he said. "His esthetic sense was outraged, he did his best to convince me that the trees were in the right place for the rest of the shrubs.

"In case you do not appreciate your father, Steve, he has an instinctive sense of what is right in landscaping. *My* esthetic sense breaks down when convenience is at stake.

"The Samantha School team would never be the same if you dropped out of the program," Mr. Grundy went on. "And that has nothing to do with esthetic sense. I remember how my grandson did exercises intended to strengthen and stretch muscles that would make him taller. So I am fully aware of the importance of height to a basketball player and to his team."

Mr. Grundy held Steve's gaze and the twinkle went from his eyes as he continued. "Now, if you do as thorough a job at grabbing rebounds as Fluorescence does at grabbing bugs and varmints that stray into our garden, everything will be fine!"

Steve stood with the other boys from Samantha School, lined up across the floor of the basketball court in Beach City Junior High gymnasium. He wondered if Red Jeffery and Mike Whitney and Dick Meredith felt the same funny emptiness inside that he did. Steve stole a glance at Winthrop Prouty. The dark-haired boy appeared perfectly at ease. Well, Prouty had been coached by a real coach. He knew what this waiting-for-a-game-to-start ritual was all about.

The team from Beach City Junior High at the other end of the court were throwing at the basket, dribbling, pivoting, making lay-up shots. It was all done smoothly and nonchalantly as though everything was a matter of course. This would not bother Prouty.

It bothered Steve Reynolds.

"Unlax!" Fred Conley looked first at Steve, then glanced swiftly at the other four boys who were in the starting lineup for Samantha School. "These guys are giving us the treatment to impress us. They're not as comfortable and unconcerned as they let on. It's their first game, too. They are as quivery inside as you are. We are as good as they are—better!

"Get the jump, Steve," Fred went on. "It shouldn't be too tough. Tap the ball to Red. Then you cut around their center while Red fakes a dribble and passes off to Prouty. If it looks clear, Win dribbles in for a lay-up. If traffic clogs things, you should be in the hole by then and Prouty passes to you. You will hand off to Prouty or Red when they cut past, or maybe fake to one or both, pivot around and sink a hook shot—whichever seems best right then."

Fred Conley looked around the group.

"The first basket won't necessarily win the game," he said. "But it will look nice and pretty on the scoreboard if we get it. And we can. Let's go!"

Steve had no trouble in outreaching the Beach City center. He pushed the ball toward the area where Red Jeffery was supposed to gather it in. One thing happened that Fred Conley and his teammates had not foreseen.

A Beach City Junior High boy jumped in front of Red Jeffery and grabbed the ball.

Steve reacted instinctively. He leaped out of the center circle, took two giant strides and overwhelmed the boy who had the ball. His long arm

slammed across the forearm of the Beach City boy and the ball dropped from his grasp. Steve pounced on the sphere, drew it back to make a pass and the whistles of both referee and umpire shrilled.

"Hacking!" The referee cried. "Foul on Number Nine, White! One shot for Number Four, Blue!"

Steve glanced down at the numeral nine on the front of his basketball shirt. He raised his hand to indicate to the scorer that he was the fouler. The teams trudged to the Beach City free throw line. Number Four, Blue stood on the free throw line, sighted, pushed a one-handed shot upward and the ball swished through the basket netting.

Beach City Junior High, 1; Samantha School, 0.

Mike Whitney threw the ball in from out of bounds beneath the basket. Winthrop Prouty took the throw-in, faked a Beach City boy beautifully and drove toward the basket dribbling fast. Dick Meredith, who was open, waved his hand frantically, but Prouty either did not see his teammate was in the clear, or chose to ignore him. He was twenty feet out when he aimed briefly, pushed a one-hander toward the basket—and the ball dropped through the netted circle without touching backboard or basket rim.

As Beach City threw the ball in bounds, Fred Conley stood on the sideline and yelled, "Defense! Get back, you guys!"

The Samantha School boys did not react

quickly enough. A Beach City boy took a pass in the open for a clear shot, but was too anxious and missed.

Steve drove in for the rebound, but unfortunately he plowed right over an opponent. He retrieved the ball, but the officials could not possibly have missed the flagrant charging foul he committed in getting to it.

Not quite five minutes of the first period had been played when the umpire called a third foul on the big boy, and then a fourth in rapid succession when Steve again barged over an opponent in going for the rebound. The big Samantha School center could have been charged with two other fouls, if the officials had been strictly technical.

Only ten seconds of playing time remained in the quarter when Steve fouled again—and that was the foul that disqualified him from further play in the game. He walked to the bench with head hanging. The Beach City boy made both free throws that had been awarded him and the scoreboard read Beach City Junior High, 8; Samantha School, 2. Six of Beach City's total had come from free throws after fouls by Steve Reynolds.

Mr. Grundy might as well have not given me the shoes, Steve thought. People would not have had time to notice whether I had shoes or not!

The final score of the game was Beach City Junior High, 38; Samantha School, 12.

CHAPTER EIGHT

Mr. Grundy Gives Advice

STEVE forgot his basketball shoes that morning. He trotted home after school to get them and, when he came back he knew from the way Fred Conley looked that something had gone on while he was away. Fred glanced toward Winthrop Prouty before he spoke.

"I still think we should work mostly on footwork and rebounding today," Fred said. "I found a drill in a book that gives practice in both."

"And I still say we need practice shooting baskets more than rebounding stuff!" Prouty shouted. "A team that makes only twelve points in a game had *better* practice shooting!"

"A team won't have a chance to shoot baskets if they don't get the ball. Most of the time rebounding is the way a team gains possession of the ball. And footwork is part of rebounding which will make—"

"—so many fouls that the other guys will swamp you with free throws!" Prouty glared at Steve. "I was open seven or eight times, too, and the big clown would not pass me the ball!"

Steve frowned. He *had* passed to Prouty. Actually, two of the fouls that had been called on him happened because he looked around for Prouty—or any teammate he could pass to—and a Beach City boy had come after the ball before he found anyone open. Then he fouled the opponent because he was so awkward and could not avoid contact. Prouty had to know that he was not being truthful.

"We also need practice in getting open," Prouty went on. "I looked for someone to pass to a lot of times and nobody was open."

"Name me one time!" Dick Meredith snorted. "You were so basket-happy that you never even looked for anyone else when you got your hands on the ball!"

"I made eight points, how many did you make? And I didn't foul out of the game!"

Fred Conley, Dick Meredith, Red Jeffery and others looked toward Steve. What goes on, he wondered. I was the guy who fouled out, not Dick. Then it hit him suddenly that Prouty was aiming all his remarks at him.

Before anyone could reply, Fred Conley took three newspaper clippings from his pocket. "These are from the *Miami Herald* sports section," he said. "I'd like to read them." He selected the one to read first.

"St. Thomas Aquinas enjoyed sweet revenge Friday by edging the Pompano Beach Golden Tornadoes, 62-60 at the Aquinas gym for the first victory over Pompano in more than a decade.

"St. Thomas Aquinas was led by forward Rich Tomaski's shooting and"—Fred glanced at Steve— "the strong rebounding of center Bert Contelino, who controlled the boards throughout the game, but especially in the final crucial minutes, and added fourteen points to the St. Thomas effort!"

Fred gave Prouty a brief look, then read from another clipping.

"Jupiter High toppled Belle Glade in a mild upset as Cochrane—their big man at 6'5", gathered in 19 rebounds and ruined Belle Glade's fast break attack."

Fred read from a third clipping.

"Vero Beach rode the rebounding of 6'7" Bob Vetti and 6'5" Book Wilson to a 67–62 basketball victory over previously unbeaten Riviera Beach Friday night.

"Wilson grabbed 22 rebounds and scored the basket that gave Vero a three-point lead in the closing minute of play. Vetti's aggressive rebounding broke up the effort of Riviera Beach Hornets' closing drive when he controlled the defensive board for Vero Beach."

Fred folded the clippings and looked steadily at Prouty while he returned them to his pocket. "Practically every account of games played in the area Friday brought out how important rebounding was to the winners," Fred said.

"Those are high school teams! They've been coached how to get open and shoot baskets!" Prouty was almost screaming. "Not a bunch of guys who—"

"Who are creating a disturbance!" Words from Miss Smith cut through Prouty's protest. The teacher had opened the door from the school building to the playground without any of the boys hearing or seeing her. "You are becoming louder and louder and the noise is disrupting the Mothers' Club meeting inside. You simply must quiet down!"

Miss Smith looked from Prouty to Fred Conley. Steve had the impression that the teacher knew there was more to this than merely a too-loud discussion. Her incisive tone left no room for doubt when she said then, "We do not expect a basketball practice to be held in Quaker-meeting-has-begun-no-more-laughing-no-more-fun atmosphere. But we

do expect you to remember that others have rights
that must be considered!"

Miss Smith looked around the group. Steve was
sure that her eyes lingered an extra moment on Fred
Conley and Winthrop Prouty. She asked, "Clear?"

"Yes, ma'am." Fred gulped. "We're sorry, Miss
Smith."

The teacher went back into the building. The
boys looked at each other.

"We're lucky she didn't kick us off the playground right now!" Whitey Kemp shot a look toward Prouty. "For sure she'll do it if she has to come
back out! Let's get with it on *some* kind of practice!"

Steve thought, that's the first time one of his
pals has gone against the grain with Prouty. But he
sure has a right to gripe about the way I let the team
down!

Steve and Fred walked together from the playground. "We showed a lot of improvement," Fred
said. "Turned out to be a good practice."

"I'm glad you gave in to Prouty and had us
shooting baskets."

"I didn't give in to anybody. A team has to
practice shooting a lot; we were going to do it anyway." Fred drew in a breath. "I just wish that Prouty
would get over acting as though he and I are in a
contest or something! As for you, Steve, you were

really grabbing rebounds, and you weren't fouling."

"Maybe I *was* fouling, if there had been a real referee."

"No. I watched you extra carefully and called everything that even looked like contact. Steve, you just have to forget the way things went at Beach City. Think positive; believe that you can move around as well as any of their guys. Trouble over there was that you were too anxious. You tried to carry the whole load, pressed and got off on the wrong foot. You can grab rebounds and dunk hook shots on those guys. I know you can!"

Fred was so intent on convincing Steve that he had merely suffered a "poor day," they were at the corner by the Reynolds home before he realized. He smote his forehead and grinned.

"And my mother gave me heck for doing this before when I was supposed to come right home!"

Fred took off at a trot.

Mr. Reynolds came from work not long after Fred had gone. "Mr. Grundy wants to see you," he told Steve. "It will take me a while to clean up before dinner. Why don't you run over there now?"

"I watched Fred Conley stand up to young Prouty," Mr. Grundy said. "I couldn't help but wonder if Win Prouty, Senior, is aware of his son's actions. Fred may not be able to demonstrate as he would like, but he surely gets the meat from what he reads and can tell your team how to do things. Just what seems to be the trouble between him and Win Prouty's son?"

Steve shifted his weight from one leg to the other. He did not know what to say. Then he blurted, "Me! Everything I do is wrong! Prouty is smoother and more clever. I'm just a thorn in the side of Fred and the team. Fred and Prouty would get along fine if it wasn't for me! Somebody ought to pull me out of Fred's hair!"

"Nonsense!"

Mr. Grundy began talking and Steve suddenly realized that he was making the same points Fred had made. Steve began to wonder if Fred had stopped and talked with Mr. Grundy. But there had not been time between Fred's leaving and Pa's coming home.

"Fred Conley is not the only one who reads," Mr. Grundy said. "Several books on basketball technique are in our library, left from years back when our grandson studied them. For instance, I read in a book entitled *How to Play Better Basketball* that pivoting, faking and feinting, stops and starts—all the moves a basketball player needs—can be learned and perfected off the basketball court. The writer advised chasing a playful dog or cat.

"Now, the first time your father brought your pet over here, I watched Fluorescence while she stalked a mouse in the vacant field adjoining our back garden. She would feint one direction, draw the mouse off-balance, then shift quickly and pounce the other way. The mouse was good, but Fluorescence was far superior.

"Nature equips animals with instinctive moves that mean life or death in the primitive world. Animals depend on them to obtain food or to keep from becoming food for others!"

Mr. Grundy chuckled and gave Steve a friendly pat. "I advise you to take Fluorescence out behind your garage and romp with her and sharpen your own moves," he said. "She can teach you a lot and add to your confidence."

CHAPTER NINE

Fluorescence Comes to Practice

STEVE followed Mr. Grundy's advice. Fluorescence seemed surprised when he took her out behind the garage and did not fasten the leash to her collar.

"Look, girl, maybe you can help the team by getting me so I'm not so awkward," he told her. "You sold yourself to Mr. Grundy, now let's see you measure up to all he said."

Steve loped away from his pet. Fluorescence needed no second invitation. She ran after him, caught up, weaved between his legs, and when Steve lunged at her, neatly sidestepped and whirled away.

"You little dickens!" Steve chased the animal.

"Mr. Grundy sure knew what he was talking about when he said you'd be naturally slippery!"

Fluorescence ran and darted and dodged and whirled. Steve failed to get near enough to his pet to lay a hand on her.

"Okay," he said finally, and waited a second or so until his chest stopped heaving and he could go on speaking. "You skunked me this time—ha, ha, sounds like I made a funny—but the way you made me look bad is not funny! Soon as I get my breath we'll have another go-around!"

The second "go-around" ended the same as the first, but Steve came closer. He was really close in several later sessions. Then came a time when Fluorescence stopped and turned another direction and his big hand was waiting. He swept her up.

"If you weren't fooling, girl, I sure must be getting better!" He grinned at his pet. "Took pretty good footwork to follow that maneuver!"

Fluorescence purred and licked his hand. He was sure that his pet was telling him as best she could how happy she was at being able to help him shed some of his awkwardness.

"The thing that defeats me," Steve told Fred as they walked from practice one afternoon, "is that I have got so I can out-smart Fluorescence sometimes. Then when I get on the basketball court, I'm still stiff and uncomfortable and clumsy."

"You just don't know how much you have improved! Man, you're getting smoother all the time!"

"I hope you aren't just giving me a line." Steve sighed. "It took me a solid week chasing Fluorescence before I could catch her once in a while. Maybe I'll finally learn to go after a rebound without slamming into the other guys when I have the ball."

"You fouled a lot less today. And I called everything real close. Man, you are going to give those junior high guys a BIG surprise when they come out here next week!"

That night after dinner, Steve's father said, "Mr. Grundy wants you to come over there this evening. He said for you to bring Fluorescence along." George Reynolds eyed his son. "Looks as though he has kind of adopted you and your pet. The way he watches you boys when you are playing back of the school! He is all wound up with you and what he refers to as 'young Conley's way of getting identity for Samantha School.'

"I don't know about basketball teams, but I know this: Mr. Grundy is a fine gentleman. If he wants you to do something—do it!"

What Mr. Grundy wanted was for Steve to leave Fluorescence overnight. "I had some special hyacinth bulbs packed ready to send a friend," he explained. "Some animal has been gnawing at them. I can find no place where a squirrel might have come from outside; there may be mice or something. I would like to turn Fluorescence loose in the barn. Incidentally, it has been interesting to see how you have improved getting around on the court. Did you follow the tip I gave you from the book?"

Steve nodded. If Mr. Grundy saw improvement, Fred Conley had not been just handing him a line. Steve felt a little empty inside, leaving his pet, but he was happy that he could do something for Mr. Grundy.

Fred Conley looked first at Winthrop Prouty and then at Steve.

Fred doesn't realize that he really bases things on Prouty, Steve thought. And that's okay. Prouty knows more about playing basketball that any of us, including Fred, no matter how much reading Fred has done.

"Okay," Fred said. "We looked real good in the drills. Now we'll work on team stuff. We'll scrimmage as if we were in a game. You second team, give the first team as bad a time as you can!"

Steve easily got the tipoff. He slanted the ball across to the left and Winthrop Prouty grabbed it. Prouty started a fast dribble, and barely glanced around. His guard was late in covering and Prouty dribbled all the way in, leaped and laid the ball against the backboard. It dropped through the netting.

"Way to go! That's dunking."

Steve yelled approval of the beautifully exe-
cuted lay-up. It happened that Fred Conley was in
his line of vision as he turned to run back on defense. He was surprised to see that Fred was scowling.

The second team tossed the ball in bounds from
beneath the basket. Two more passes and then one
went wild. Dick Meredith intercepted. Dick flipped
the ball to Prouty near midcourt, cut around a second team player and clapped his hands signaling
Prouty for a return pass.

Again Prouty scarcely looked for an open teammate, ignoring Dick completely. Prouty dribbled,
faked a second team player to the left across the ten-
second line, then darted to the right and drove for
the basket. He leaped and put the ball against the
board—but the momentum of his drive caused the
shot to hit the backboard too hard and bounce to the
front edge of the basket rim. It skittered off to one
side.

Steve and the second team center went after
the rebound. Both clutched the ball. Fred Conley
shrilled his whistle. "Held ball," Fred cried. "Jump
at the free throw line."

"You think you're the only guy on the team
when you get the ball, Prouty!" Dick yelled. "I was
wide open!"

"The name of the game is scoring." Prouty shrugged. "How can you score without making baskets? I had a clear path for a drive."

"Yah! And you blew it! Might be that another guy could make a basket besides you, too!"

Fred Conley said, "Win, you didn't look to see if anyone was open for a pass either time you got the ball. That's no way to get teamwork!"

"Teamwork, shmeemwork! Get off my back and get on with practice!"

Fred tossed the ball high between Steve and the second team center. Steve tipped the sphere to Mike Whitney, faked to the right, pivoted smoothly and fooled his cover completely. He then angled toward the sideline and took Mike's pass near the boundary. Suddenly a small animal with white markings on black fur dashed at Steve, whirled and skittered away. Steve nearly stumbled.

The furry little animal caught sight of Fred, recognized a friend and darted at him.

"A skunk!" The shout came from Winthrop Prouty. "Everybody stand back!"

He started toward the furry animal. "That's no skunk, that's Fluorescence!" Fred cried. "Stay away, she won't harm anybody!"

"I know how to handle a skunk!" Prouty kept coming toward the animal warily. "You get in a good kick before she can let you have it!"

Fluorescence must have thought that he was another to frolic with as she had been doing with her master. She darted toward Prouty. He kicked at her. The animal swerved, easily avoiding the kick. Then Steve had Prouty by the arm. He spun Prouty away from his pet, not gently.

Prouty glared, tried again to get at Fluorescence. Steve grabbed the front of Prouty's basketball jersey in one huge hand and held him at arm's length.

Flailing his fists, beating at Steve's arm, Prouty yelled, "Let me go, you big jerk! That skunk will douse all of us!"

Steve just shook Prouty and shook him and shook him. Winthrop Prouty, Jr. was as helpless in the grasp of Steve as a mouse would have been with Fluorescence.

Fred was chasing Fluorescence and she dodged away still playing her games. Suddenly she dodged right into the hands of Mr. Grundy and was whisked from the concrete. Mr. Grundy—panting and with hair awry—cuddled Fluorescence in his arms.

"I'm terribly sorry." Mr. Grundy held Steve's gaze. "She found the hole that field mice were using to get into my barn. She was watching it when I went out there a while ago. I left the door open when I went to call your father to cover the hole.

"Quite evidently Fluorescence followed me

from the barn, saw you down here and came to help you practice. It took much longer for me to scramble down the hill than it did your pet!"

"Pet!" Winthrop Prouty almost snarled the word. "Now we have to dodge a skunk because the big clown has one for a *pet!*"

Prouty looked around at his cronies. "If a guy has to be a skunk-lover to play for this crummy team, I've had it!"

He started from the basketball court. "Are you guys with me?"

"Hold it!" The sharpness of Mr. Grundy's tone startled Steve. Mr. Grundy had always spoken gently and softly before, but he went on in the same tone. "I would advise all of you to think a little before doing anything rash!"

The effect of Mr. Grundy's words was amazing. Boys who had moved as though to follow Prouty now stood still. Prouty seemed to be momentarily frozen as he stared at the cement surface of the basketball court.

Then he raised his eyes, looked defiantly at the elderly gentleman, turned angrily, intending to stalk from the court—and almost barged full tilt into Miss Smith.

No one had heard or noticed Miss Smith when she came from the building. Steve was not alone in staring at the teacher.

"Winthrop, go to my room!" Miss Smith's tone

left no doubt that she had the situation well in hand. "Fred, please come with me."

She looked toward Mr. Grundy and her words were as much demand as request when she said, "Keep things going a few minutes, Mr. Grundy? Fred and Winthrop will not be long!"

CHAPTER TEN

The Name of the Game

STEVE watched Mr. Grundy. He would have had difficulty in explaining why he was so proud of his elderly friend. Steve did not miss the twinkle in Mr. Grundy's eyes as he said:

"It could be that I arranged all this so Miss Smith would leave me in charge. I must admit that I have had a secret desire to be down here helping coach you fellows. I suppose that traces back a few years to when my grandson spent vacations with me and I learned about basketball."

Mr. Grundy chuckled.

"Anyway, somewhere along the line I was thoroughly bitten by the basketball bug," he said. "My grandson is doing all right, too. He is first string center and second high scorer for the North State University freshman team."

Mr. Grundy looked briefly at Steve. He said, "I don't think I need to say much about the doctrine that Fred Conley has been preaching to you boys— the name of the game in today's basketball is control of the backboards. It is a big man's game from pro-teams down through college, high school, junior high school and as far as you go."

Steve saw Mike Whitney glance toward Whitey Kemp. Mike ran his fingers through his hair.

"Sir," Mike said, "you say the name of the game is control of the backboards. Okay, getting the ball on rebounds is very important. But we also hear that the name of the game is scoring. A guy gets confused."

"Name of the game." Mr. Grundy repeated the phrase as he inclined his head. "I suspect that anyone trying to make his point is apt to say the name of the game is whatever he is plugging for. Of course, the name of the game is basketball, which includes many skills. I also suspect that young Conley has told you much the same."

Again Mr. Grundy inclined his head indicating full agreement.

"I have watched every practice so closely that I feel a personal interest in your team. Nobody playing basketball was ever harmed by hearing over and over that control of the backboards is of vital importance."

This time Steve was sure that Mr. Grundy eyed him a little longer when he looked around.

"Now," the elderly gentleman said, "young Prouty claims that the name of the game is scoring. Some might say that the name of the game is teamwork—defense—playmaking—fast break—spirit—you name it and there will be others who will stoutly defend and support whatever claim is made.

"A team must have playmakers to start things rolling so that we get a shot at the other fellow's basket. There must be shooters who can sink that round thing in the bucket!"

Mr. Grundy laughed whole-heartedly and said, "I wish my grandson could hear how he has corrupted me! One thing—name of the game or whatever—we need to keep our big man in the game. And his little pet has done more than any of us to improve her master's footwork and perhaps keep him from making so many fouls."

Mr. Grundy put Fluorescence on the concrete and fastened her leash to her collar.

"But she really can't help right now. All right, let's keep in mind that we are going to make Beach City Junior High respect Samantha School. So let us continue the practice as Miss Smith suggested."

Steve wondered if other boys were playing as he was—with part of his attention on the door to the school building. Miss Smith had been right when she said that Fred and Prouty would not be long. They reappeared in ten minutes.

Winthrop Prouty looked deflated and yet not defeated. He glanced toward Mr. Grundy, met the man's gaze for a moment, then dropped his eyes.

"Sometimes we have to learn the hard way." Mr. Grundy made it clear that he was talking directly to Winthrop Prouty, Jr. "You needed to be made aware of a few facts. Whatever bitterness you feel should be aimed at me. I hope the air has been cleared and that all of you will work for the good of the team."

Mr. Grundy pulled at Fluorescence's leash until he could reach her, picked up the animal and carried her away from the basketball court.

Dick Meredith watched them go. "Fluorescence," he said thoughtfully. "Fluoro to me." He turned back to the boys. "Now what?" he asked.

"We'll scrimmage a while," answered Fred. "Same guys in the same spots."

Steve pushed the ball toward Winthrop Prouty on the tipoff. Prouty darted for the basket apparently bent on driving all the way in. Suddenly he stopped as though something had occurred to him. He heaved the ball in the general direction of Steve.

It was not a good pass. Even Steve's extra long arms could not reach the ball.

"Second team out of bounds," Fred called. "Let's watch the passing!"

The second team passed and dribbled, working the ball upcourt. Prouty darted toward a dribbler, feinted the second team man into breaking his dribble. He attempted to make a pass but his pivot foot dragged too far and Fred blew his whistle. "Progress!" he called. "First team out!"

Dick Meredith stood with the ball beyond the side boundary. Prouty dashed across the ten-second line and Dick snapped a pass to him, then cut diagonally for the basket. It seemed that Prouty was going to dribble all the way in but he faked cleverly and made a bounce pass around a second team player driving at him. The ball led Meredith perfectly.

"Deadeye Dick" grabbed the sphere, leaped and laid the ball feather-soft against the backboard. It slanted down through the netted ring.

"Beautiful!" Fred shouted. "That's teamwork!"

Dick Meredith ran past Prouty as they dropped back on defense. "Right on the money, Win!" Dick gave Prouty a pat on the hip. "A guy can't miss the bucket when that round thing comes to him like that!"

Twenty-eight seconds later Dick Meredith was scowling. He passed to Prouty, eluded his guard with fine footwork and broke clear at the foul circle. He yelled for the ball. Prouty did not pass; instead, he shot from thirty feet out.

The ball dropped through the hoop, dead center. But Dick Meredith was muttering and shaking his head as he ran back for defense.

In spite of this, Steve felt as though Winthrop Prouty was trying for teamplay, even though he sometimes reverted to the Prouty-do-it-all business. At the end of the scrimmage, Steve believed it was as good a practice as they had ever had—and better than most.

Steve walked with Fred from the school. "All right, give," Steve said. "Prouty seemed pretty tamed when you came back. What happened?"

"Well, Miss Smith did not fool around. She had talked with Prouty's old man over the phone last night. Mr. Grundy and Mr. Prouty are in some business together, I guess. Anyway, from the way Miss Smith laid things on the barrelhead to Win, Mr. Grundy must have laid things on the line to Win's father.

"Mr. Prouty told Miss Smith that he did not want Win thinking that he was something special. He had been acting like a spoiled brat and he—Mr. Prouty, that is—wanted him cut down to size."

Fred stopped and let out a whistle.

"Man, if anybody thought Miss Smith hasn't

known what has been going on between you and Prouty, they have eighty-two more thinks coming!"

"What do you mean, what's been going on between me and Prouty? There's nothing been going on, 'cept he'd like to play center, I guess," objected Steve. "For sure I haven't aimed to have any goings-on between us!"

"Well, maybe I didn't say that right." Fred shrugged. "What I meant was that Miss Smith named a half dozen little items, digs that Prouty has made about lunk and stepladder and big clown, times when he has shot off his mouth at basketball practices. What she called his 'general pettishness because he has been pushed off a pedestal he seemed to consider his natural right.' Man, she nailed him to the wall good!"

"She thanked me for keeping quiet about Fluorescence being your pet," Fred went on. "And she asked me to let you know she liked the way you handled Prouty when he went after Fluorescence. Miss Smith saw the whole show from the window."

They walked a little distance in silence. Then Fred asked, "What about Mr. Grundy after Miss Smith carted Win and me off?"

"He didn't mention Prouty," Steve said. "I guess he was trying to keep everything from being too sticky. But, boy, he said a plenty! You think Miss Smith is something for knowing what went on—

that's really part of her job. The way Mr. Grundy knew so much about what went on with the team is something else!"

Steve repeated Mr. Grundy's discussion almost word for word.

"Looks as though you could say the name of the game for Mr. Grundy is putting on the pressure when it's needed," Fred said. "The old gent does not throw his weight around, but he has more influence than anybody else I can think of."

Fred sighed. "Take all that has been said and things that have happened," he said, "and shake them all together and it comes out that the name of the game for all of us is to show those junior high guys a lot of basketball when they come out here!"

CHAPTER ELEVEN

Samantha School Versus Beach City Junior High

THE line of Beach City Junior High players stretched across the playground basketball court. They wore bright orange jerseys with blue numerals on front and back. Their pants were brilliant blue with orange piping down the sides.

"They sure look like a basketball team," Steve said.

"*Teams*, you mean!" Dick Meredith shook his head. "They have twenty guys dressed to play—*twenty*, count 'em! And those uniforms make our white jerseys and khaki gym pants look kind of back-country. But the scoreboard doesn't pay off on just snazzy outfits!"

Dick glanced along the short line of ten Samantha School players who were shooting baskets in the pre-game warmup. Winthrop Prouty was at the far end. He took brief aim at the basket and arched a shot. The ball came down and swished the netting without touching rim or backboard.

"We can take these city boys," Dick said. "If we play teamwork—and you don't foul out as you did in the other game!"

"I don't think I will. Fred and Mr. Grundy and Fluorescence and—well, everybody has helped me." Steve glanced toward Winthrop Prouty. "He is plenty good," the tall boy said. "Even while he has been trying to—to—well, I guess you'd say reform —Prouty's cleverness and smoothness show up the rest of us. You have to say that he *has* been trying!"

"Yeah, I'll give him that." Dick nodded. "But that old business about a leopard changing his spots bothers me. Prouty had *better* change his spots!"

The game began. Steve outreached the Beach City center for the opening tipoff. He slanted the ball back and to the right. Dick Meredith grabbed it but before he could pass or dribble, a Beach City boy tied him up. A whistle shrilled and the referee indicated a held ball, a jump between Meredith and the Beach City boy.

Prouty came over to Steve. "I was out there

alone," Prouty complained. "If you had tipped it to me, I could have gone in for a lay-up!"

Steve said nothing. Dick Meredith glared at Prouty. "So, this leopard doesn't even want to change his spots!" Meredith said.

The Beach City boy outjumped Meredith but Red Jeffery flashed in front of the player in orange and blue who was about to take the tip. Red flipped a quick pass to Mike Whitney. Win Prouty tore for the free-throw circle and was momentarily open. But Mike saw the defensive player closing on Prouty. Mike dribbled three times, then whipped the ball to Steve as the tall boy crossed the free-throw line.

Steve faked right then pivoted left and the Beach City player attempting to guard him was lost. Steve dunked the ball into the basket.

Samantha School, 2; Beach City, o.

Beach City threw in from beneath the basket. It was a wild pass and Dick Meredith intercepted short of the ten-second line. Prouty and Mike Whitney were open. Dick passed to Whitney. Mike dribbled twice and passed to Prouty as the Samantha star forward broke around a guard and Prouty made the lay-up good.

Samantha School, 4; Beach City, o.

Less than twenty seconds later, Mike Whitney snagged another poor Beach City pass, dribbled across the ten-second line while Prouty, Dick Meredith and Steve raced for the Samantha scoring area.

Beach City players crowded Prouty and Meredith. Mike whizzed the ball to Steve. The Samantha School's center might have tried a shot, but his guard was in front, leaping to block, and Steve passed off to Prouty.

Prouty had to hurry to get the ball away before his guard reached him, and the shot was wide. The ball bounced off the rim. Steve's hands were far above the Beach City center's as they both went up for the rebound. Steve slapped the ball over the basket rim and Samantha School had another two points.

Samantha School, 6; Beach City, 0.

Beach City called time-out. The Samantha School boys gathered around Fred Conley as the Beach City boys surrounded their coach in front of their bench.

"Great going, guys!" Fred Conley was jubilant. "Their coach started a team of seventh graders—but I'll bet they'll have their regular eighth and ninth grade starters in before long!"

Steve suddenly understood why everything he had done so far had clicked so well. The Beach City boys were not the same team that had played before. He wondered if he would show to such advantage when the Beach City coach put his regular five into the game.

Although no change had been made in the

Beach City lineup when play was resumed after the time-out, it became clear that the coach had told the Beach City boys something. They passed better. They worked the ball down the floor into shooting range, but missed a basket-try.

Steve took the rebound. A Beach City boy fouled him. Steve made the free throw and with the score 7–0 against Beach City, their coach sent five players off the bench to report to the scorer.

Substitutes could not come into the game until the ball was dead and Beach City did not call time-out while they had possession of the ball. One of their boys tried a long shot, missed, and the ball bounced off the backboard into the hands of Mike Whitney.

Mike whipped a long pass to Dick Meredith at the center line. Win Prouty raced down the opposite side and the fast-break play caught Beach City with but one man back to cover two opponents.

He committed himself going after Meredith and could do nothing when Meredith flipped a pass to Prouty. Prouty had an easy lay-up chance, but banged the ball too hard against the backboard. Steve ran in, leaped high and again tapped the sphere into the basket.

A Beach City boy made frantic signs to the referee for time-out. A new team came on the floor for Beach City, faced now with a 9–0 deficit.

The second quarter of play was different.

Beach City was a well-coached team. Their first team was bigger than the Samantha School boys, except for Steve. They were more clever at footwork and smoother ball-handlers, except for Winthrop Prouty.

They scored the first Beach City basket twelve seconds after play resumed. Mike Whitney passed long after the basket, attempting another fast break. This time the Beach City guard played perfect defense. He held Prouty and Meredith from getting into good position until help came. Prouty shot from the corner, missed, and the Beach City center outmaneuvered Steve to grab the rebound.

Coming down with the ball, the Beach City boy dribbled toward the corner, pivoted and hooked a shot over his shoulder. Steve fouled him, the basket was good, and the Beach City boy made the free throw for a three-point play.

Samantha School, 9; Beach City, 5.

Suddenly the boys in orange and blue were back in the ball game. That was when Winthrop Prouty seemed to feel that he was called upon to take charge. He sunk a long shot from thirty-five feet out. Score: 11–5 for Samantha School.

Sharp Beach City passing worked the ball in for a high-percentage try and the shot was good. Score: 11–7.

The pass-in was to Steve. He heard Prouty yell,

"Here! I'm open!" Steve passed to Prouty and headed for the basket area.

Meredith and Red Jeffery were open now, but Prouty did not pass. He tried to dribble in, had the ball neatly snared away by a Beach City guard. Then the boy in orange and blue double-dribbled and Dick Meredith took the ball out of bounds.

Prouty faked his guard left then dashed right, toward Meredith. Dick ignored him and passed to Red Jeffery instead. It was not a good pass. Before Red could gain firm possession he was tied up in a jump ball.

Play seesawed. Jeffery scored a field goal; Meredith was fouled and dropped both his free throws through the netting; Mike Whitney rang up a long shot. But while these six points were being accumulated by Samantha School, Beach City put three field goals and one free throw through the Samantha basket.

Steve made the foul that gave Beach City the successful free throw.

Three seconds before the end of the period, the big Samantha School center was charged with his third foul. The free throw was missed, but Steve was not in a comfortable position, foul-wise. He knew that two of the fouls marked against him came from careless, blundering, clumsy play. Stepladder Steve he thought. I'm letting the team down, and I've got to snap out of it!

When the timekeeper signaled the end of the second quarter, the score was Samantha School, 17; Beach City, 14.

"We blew a good lead," Fred Conley said after the team came off the court. "All I can say is play as you started out and you can beat these guys, regulars or seventh graders!" He glanced toward Winthrop Prouty. "But we have to play as a *team*—or they'll chase us off our own court the second half!"

The third quarter was barely under way when a Beach City shot bounced high off the rim of the basket. Steve was guarding the opposing center in the foul circle. Beach City's "big man" faked right and drew Steve that way for just the vital instant he needed to dart around the Samantha School center and gain position for the rebound.

They went up after the ball together, banged hard in the air. Steve knew his fingers jabbed into his opponent's face. He did not know he had stuck a finger into the Beach City boy's eye until the referee blew his whistle and motioned the Beach City coach to come from the bench.

"There was no foul," the referee said while the coach examined his player's eye. "Both boys were after the ball, legitimately."

"After all, they're only kids," the coach said. "You have to expect a certain amount of awkwardness. I am not squawking foul!"

Steve felt terrible. If he had not been fooled by his opponent's clever footwork, there would have been no collision. He could easily have been called for a foul, too. Stepladder Steve was still letting his team down.

CHAPTER TWELVE

Something Smells—
and Not Fluorescence!

BEACH CITY played relentless, aggressive basketball, trying hard to keep the pressure on Samantha School all the time. But as their coach said, they *were* only youngsters. They made mistakes, and Steve was a tower of strength for his team.

Nobody kept track of the number of rebounds the big boy snared. There was no record of the passes and handoffs he made to Dick Meredith, Win Prouty and Red Jeffery that resulted in Samantha shots at the basket. Mike Whitney could have testified to a lot of rebounds Steve took off the Beach City board and passed out to him.

Anyone who knew basketball would have recognized that Steve kept his team in the game. But Beach City ground down the Samantha School margin until near the end of the third quarter they went into the lead for the first time, 27–26.

That was when Winthrop Prouty showed that he had NOT reformed.

Mike Whitney passed in to Red Jeffery after the basket that put Beach City ahead. Steve ran to take position in the foul circle and Dick Meredith slanted toward the corner of the court on his side. Jeffery passed to Prouty and darted down the line on the opposite side.

Any of the trio could have been passed to—one of them SHOULD have been passed to—but Prouty kept the ball. He dribbled until a Beach City player pinched him to the sideline, then shot from forty feet out.

He missed badly. The ball bounced off the rim into the hands of a Beach City guard. He passed quickly to a mate near the center of the court and two players wearing orange and blue bore down on Mike Whitney.

Mike finally had to commit himself and the one left unguarded took a sharp pass and counted an easy lay-up.

29–26, now.

Mike again passed in to Jeffery. This time the redhead shied the ball to Meredith. Dick dribbled twice, threw a good pass to Steve. He saw Prouty cutting for the basket, handed off and Prouty made the lay-up. 29–28.

Prouty intercepted a ragged Beach City pass fifteen seconds later. He was barely on the front-court side of the center line, but he fired a long effort. It missed. Steve came down with the rebound, dribbled toward the corner to get out of the heavy traffic, then aimed a pass toward Dick Meredith.

Winthrop Prouty dashed across and grabbed the ball. He did not even look to see whether a teammate was open. He dribbled twice, swerved away from a defensive man and let fire another long try. The throw was far short.

Beach City's fast-break play again caught Mike Whitney alone in the back court with three opponents racing for the basket area. Steve sped to help the guard. The three-on-one setup overwhelmed Mike before Steve got there, and when Steve leaped too late to block a shot, he slammed into the shooter and was called for a charging foul.

The free throw was good. The three-point play increased the score to Beach City, 32; Samantha School, 28.

Beach City counted another field goal seconds before the end of the quarter. It came as the result of Prouty attempting to dribble around an opponent, and having the ball neatly snaked away. A fast pass followed, and a fifteen-foot shot swished through the net.

Beach City, 34; Samantha School, 28. End of the third quarter.

Fred Conley looked levelly at Winthrop Prouty when the boys gathered in front of the bench. "It's supposed to be Beach City versus Samantha School *team!*" Fred said. "Not Win Prouty versus Beach City. Your hogging the ball cost us our momentum! You're losing the game for us!"

"You're crazy! We wouldn't be *in* the game if it wasn't for me!" Prouty glared at Fred, then shifted his eyes to Steve. "We lost our momentum when Big Lunk fouled. He must have been playing with his skunk—the way his playing smells!"

"Something smells, all right!" Dick Meredith snorted. "But it's not Steve's play. *You stink out loud, Prouty!* If I was Fred, I'd yank you out of the game!"

"He can't! You guys wouldn't have a chance! The way Conley babies that big jerk! Between him and that stinking skunk, we're lucky to—"

Prouty got no farther. Steve's big hand shot out and grabbed Prouty's jersey front. He yanked Prouty close.

"I reckon that's enough!" Steve spoke in a soft drawl, but there was nothing soft nor mild about his expression. "Y'all call me anything you like, but lay off Fred and lay off my pet. You hear!"

"Miss Smith could not be here," Fred said. "She told me to keep you in line, Prouty. I *could* take you out of the lineup!"

Steve said, "Leave him in. Give him another chance to play basketball the way he must have been taught when he had coaching at camp!"

The timekeeper sounded the start of the final quarter. "Same guys in there as have been in there," Fred said. "Keep in mind that you are in foul trouble, Steve. We will really be sunk if you foul out!"

Steve did not realize that something had happened, that the team was looking toward him as leader. The big boy played as hard as he could.

Whether because Beach City grew complacent and let down, or because Samantha School fought harder, the six-point lead gradually melted.

Dick Meredith shot a rim-bouncer and Steve tipped the ball through the circle; Red Jeffery broke away to take a pass and score—and the pass was made by Prouty—before Beach City registered a field goal. Their basket made the score 36–32.

They traded baskets. 38–34. Then both teams struck a "cold spell" when nothing thrown toward the baskets went in. Prouty attempted to bat the ball away from a dribbler and fouled. The free throw was good. 39–34.

Prouty scowled toward Steve. "I thought I could get it," he growled.

Steve nodded. "We'll get it back," he said.

The game went on. During time-out for a two-shot foul awarded a Beach City shooter, Dick Meredith asked the timekeeper how much playing time remained.

"One minute and thirteen seconds!"

The Beach City boy missed both free throw attempts. Red Jeffery eluded his man, went in and grabbed a high-bouncing rebound, then dribbled the length of the floor, weaving around defensive players, to make his lay-up. Score: 39–36 for Beach City.

Dick Meredith sunk a corner shot. 39–38.

Beach City made a too-hurried pass in and Mike Whitney got the ball. Seconds went by while Samantha School maneuvered. Then Steve feinted his cover off-balance and broke into the clear. Prouty, who had the ball, hesitated a fraction of a second, glancing toward the basket before he passed, and the pass to Steve was late. The Beach City center dashed in front of Steve and intercepted.

He drilled a pass to a mate at the center line, and that boy zipped the ball to another orange-and-blue clad player breaking for the basket. The lay-up was good. Score: Beach City, 41; Samantha School, 38.

Prouty looked stricken. Steve took a pass and was tied up at the foul circle. He signaled that he would tip the ball Prouty's way. Easily getting the tip, Steve slanted the sphere to the dark-haired forward. He saw that Prouty was a step ahead of his guard and yelled, "Shoot!"

Prouty was startled, but aimed briefly and dropped a twelve-foot one-hander through the netting.

41–40!

Beach City took their time in throwing the ball in and passed twice before crossing the ten-second line. All they needed to do was to keep Samantha School from gaining possession of the ball. Steve crowded their center, dropped away as though going after the player with the ball, then pivoted and lunged back as a pass was made to the center. One huge hand deflected the pass.

Steve pounced at the ball like a big cat. He had it thirty feet from the basket. In the edge of his vision he saw the timekeeper with eyes glued to his stopwatch, holding his gun high ready to fire.

Steve drilled a pass to Prouty, standing near the sideline twenty-five feet from the basket. "Sink it!" Steve yelled. "Figure it's all you need in a game of 21! Shoot, y'all!"

The ball had barely arched from Prouty's hands when the timer's gun fired. The game was over. The ball slanted off the backboard behind the basket, hit the outside edge of the rim, rolled twice around the circle—and dropped outside the basket.

Final score: Beach City Junior High, 41; Samantha School, 40.

Every Samantha School boy felt mighty low as they trooped from the court. Winthrop Prouty brushed the back of his hand across his eyes, but they still glistened with unshed tears. The coach of Beach City Junior High came across the basketball court.

"Get your chins off your shoelaces," he said. "You fellows have nothing to be down about, and believe me we are tickled to pieces to escape with a win of any kind!"

He slapped Steve on the back. "Great game, Reynolds! If you were on my squad I would think seriously about winning the County Junior High Tournament!"

Then he put an arm around Fred Conley's shoulders. "You did a grand job—Coach! I will be in touch with Miss Smith. We want to play you fellows three or four times before the county tournament. I can't think of a better way to sharpen our game than to tangle with your gang!"

Win Prouty was standing near Steve when the Beach City coach left.

"Dick was right," Prouty muttered. "Something

did smell and it was not Fluorescence! You showed me up!"

He looked up at Steve, swallowed, then went on. "I guess Fred was right when he said you were what Samantha School needed," Prouty said. "I couldn't have done what you did. I would have shot, even if you had been right under the basket! And I called you 'Lunk' and 'Stepladder' and—and—well, it won't be easy, but a guy named Prouty is going to try to be for the team like you are! If I ever make another crack about you or your pet, belt me!"

"He should!" Dick Meredith nodded emphatically.

"You'd better mean what you say, Win," Red Jeffery commented. "We'll be right here to remind you!"

Mike Whitney said, "I hope I'm around so I can remind *you*, Big Boy!"

Steve looked down at Prouty. It took a lot of courage for a feller to chew himself out like Prouty had. Steve glanced toward Fred Conley who was looking anxiously from Prouty to him. Steve grinned at Fred, then switched the grin to Prouty.

"Kain't see any reason for us to belt each other," he drawled, with the "kain't" deliberately exaggerated. "Might be 'Stepladder Steve' and "Winner Win' can help Samantha School belt the other fellers when we play again!"

"Yea-a-a! . . . And how!" . . . Boys released

pent-up feelings in a burst of shouts. "We'll belt 'em good! . . . We'll climb Stepladder Steve and win with Win and him!"

Steve felt good. A feller even liked a name such as Stepladder when his teammates made things clear like now.